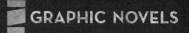

Prophets, Captives, and the Kingdom Rebuilt

2 Kings-Nehemiah

D0109156

Series Editor: Bud Rogers
Edited by Brett Burner and JS Earls
Story by Young Shin Lee
Art by Jung Sun Hwang

ZONDERVAN

ZONDERVAN.com/
AUTHORTRACKER
follow your favorite authors

ROCKFORD PUBLIC LIBRARY

SECOND KINGS
PART 2

REMEMBER! FORTY DAYS!

DON'T FORGET!

YOU'LL BE DESTROYED!

I MEAN IT!!!

THIS PROPHET MUST BE RIGHT. WE DO SIN TOO MUCH.

WE SHOULD PRAY TO GOD AND ASK FOR FORGIVENESS.

YES, WE MUST HUMBLE OURSELVES AND ASK FOR GOD'S MERCY!

O LORD! PLEASE FORGIVE US! WE'LL BE GOOD!

PALACE

WHAT? THE PEOPLE ARE PRAYING?

SOUNDS GOOD TO ME! TELL EVERYONE TO FAST AND PRAY THAT GOD WILL HAVE MERCY ON US!

ALTHOUGH I TRIED EVERYTHING TO SAVE OUR MARRIAGE, I FAILED. I STARTED TO COMPLAIN TO GOD.

LAST YEAR'S DISHES

BUT I STILL HOPED WE COULD STAY TOGETHER.

NOTHING'S CHANGED!

THEN I HAD AN IDEA...

FIRST OBSTACLE: BARBED WIRE!

SECOND OBSTACLE: HIGH WALL!

THIS'LL KEEP HER IN!

ALL RIGHT, NOW LET'S GET BACK TO THE HISTORY OF THE SOUTHERN KINGDOM OF JUDAH AND THE NORTHERN KINGDOM OF ISRAEL.

UZZIAH, WHO SUCCEEDED HIS FATHER AMAZIAH -- THE KING, NOT THE PRIEST -- AT THE AGE OF SIXTEEN, RULED JUDAH FOR FIFTY-TWO YEARS.

HE WAS CALLED *Azariah* WHEN HE WAS YOUNG, THEN *Uzziah* WHEN HE BECAME KING.

EARLY ON, HE WAS ASSISTED BY THE PROPHET ZECHARIAH AND FOLLOWED THE WILL OF GOD...

AFTER THE DEATH OF ZECHARIAH, JUDAH BECAME WEALTHY, AND KING UZZIAH GREW PRIDEFUL.

OLD KING UZZIAH.

AH, THE GOOD OLD DAYS.

I DID MANY GREAT THINGS FOR GOD! I SHOULD GO TO THE TEMPLE AND BURN SOME INCENSE.

GASP!

GOD HAS PUNISHED THE KING BY TURNING HIM INTO A LEPER!

EVENTUALLY KING UZZIAH DIED, AND BECAUSE OF HIS LEPROSY HE WASN'T BURIED WITH HIS FOREFATHERS.

AHAZ, THE GRANDSON OF UZZIAH, LATER BECAME THE NEW KING OF JUDAH.

MY LIFE'S GOAL IS TO FOLLOW BAAL.

MY KING. THE PROPHET OF BAAL IS HERE.

ISRAEL LASTED FOR THREE YEARS, BUT FINALLY FELL TO THE ASSYRIAN ARMY. THE KINGDOM OF ISRAEL, WHICH BEGAN WITH JEROBOAM OVER TWO HUNDRED YEARS AGO, WAS DESTROYED.

THE KINGS AND PROPHETS OF ISRAEL

KINGS	PROPHETS	PERIOD
JEROBOAM I		930-909 B.C.
BAASHA		908-886 B.C.
OMRI		885-874 B.C.
	ELIJAH	875-848 B.C.
AHAB		874-853 B.C.
JORAM		852-841 B.C.
	ELISHA	848-797 B.C.
JEHU		841-814 B.C.
JEHOAHAZ		814-798 B.C.
	JONAH	800-750 B.C.
JEHOASH		798-782 B.C.
JEROBOAM II		793-753 B.C.
	AMOS	760-750 B.C.
ZECHARIAH		753-752 B.C.
SHALLUM		752 B.C.
MENAHEM		752-742 B.C.
	HOSEA	750-715 B.C.
PEKAH		752-732 B.C.
PEKAHIAH		742-740 B.C.
HOSHEA		732-722 B.C.

WHAT? WE'RE BEING ATTACKED BY AN UNKNOWN ARMY?!?

NONE CAN DEFEAT OUR ASSYRIAN ARMY! CRUSH THEM!!!

AUGH!

HEL-LP!

NOOOO!!!

THE NEXT MORNING...

WHAT HAPPENED? NO ENEMY BODIES? ONLY ONE HUNDRED AND EIGHTY-FIVE THOUSAND OF OURS?

THIS IS AWFUL! LET'S HURRY BACK TO ASSYRIA!!!

EVEN MORE DISASTER WAS WAITING FOR KING SENNACHERIB IN ASSYRIA...

HE WAS KILLED BY HIS SONS WHEN HE RETURNED.

WHERE DID I GO WRONG?

I AM NOW KING AFTER KILLING OUR FATHER!

WHAT? NO, I AM NOW KING!

WHO WOULD DARE OPPOSE THE ARMY OF THE ONE TRUE GOD?

LISTEN! THIS IS THE FAITH OF JUDAH! BECAUSE OF YOUR UNFAITHFULNESS, GOD WILL DESTROY YOU LIKE THIS BROKEN JAR!

WHAP!

THAT'S IT! I CAN'T TAKE HIM ANYMORE!

CLINK!

WHAT WILL HAPPEN TO ME AND MY COUNTRY?

IT WILL BE DESTROYED, AND YOU WILL BE TAKEN CAPTIVE.

AT LEAST I WON'T BE KILLED...

GO LIVE IN THE CENTER OF TOWN; I'LL SEND FOOD TO YOU EVERY DAY.

HOW CAN JEREMIAH BE KEPT COMFORTABLE WHEN TIME AND AGAIN HE HAS SAID WE WILL BE DESTROYED?

WE SHOULD GET THE KING'S APPROVAL TO KILL JEREMIAH.

WE CAN'T LET THIS JEREMIAH -- THE ONE WHO SAYS WE ARE ALL GOING TO DIE -- GO ON LIVING.

LET US KILL HIM!

WELL... UM... OKAY.

THE KINGS AND PROPHETS OF JUDAH

KINGS	PROPHETS	PERIOD
REHOBOAM		930-913 B.C.
ASA		910-869 B.C.
JEHOSHAPHAT		872-848 B.C.
JEHORAM		853-841 B.C.
ATHALIAH		841-835 B.C.
JOASH		835-796 B.C.
UZZIAH		792-740 B.C.
JOTHAM		750-735 B.C.
AHAZ		735-715 B.C.
HEZEKIAH		715-686 B.C.
	ISAIAH	740-681 B.C.
MANASSEH		697-642 B.C.
JOSIAH		640-609 B.C.
	JEREMIAH	626-585 B.C.
JEHOAHAZ		609 B.C.
JEHOIAKIM		609-598 B.C.
JEHOIACHIN		598-597 B.C.
ZEDEKIAH		597-586 B.C.

END OF SECOND KINGS

THE PROPHETS

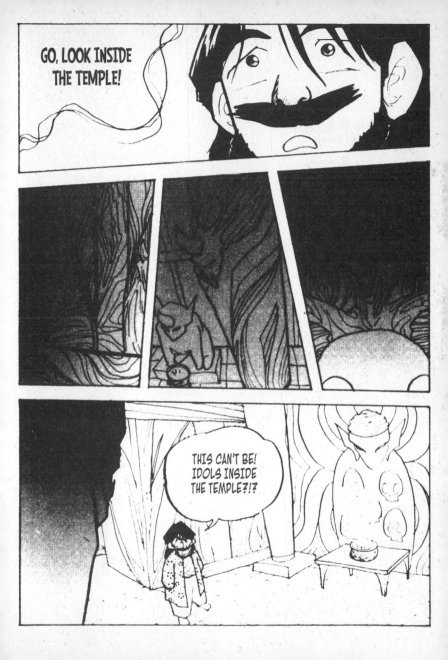

OoOoOoH...!

GOD! WILL YOU REALLY DESTROY ISRAEL THAT WAY?

YES! THEIR SINS ARE EXCEEDINGLY GREAT. I WILL BRING DOWN ON THEM WHAT THEY HAVE DONE!

ACCORDING TO GOD'S WILL, JUDAH WAS DESTROYED IN 586 B.C.

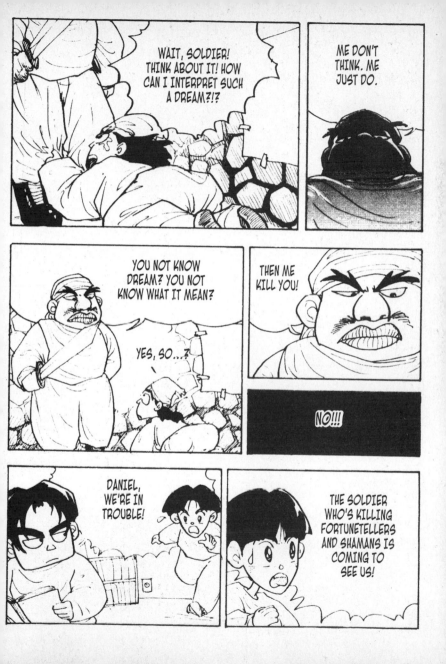

KING NEBUCHADNEZZAR DREAMT OF A LARGE STATUE. THE STATUE'S HEAD WAS GOLD, THE ARMS WERE SILVER, THE STOMACH AND THIGHS WERE BRONZE, THE CALVES WERE IRON, AND THE FEET WERE A MIXTURE OF IRON AND CLAY.

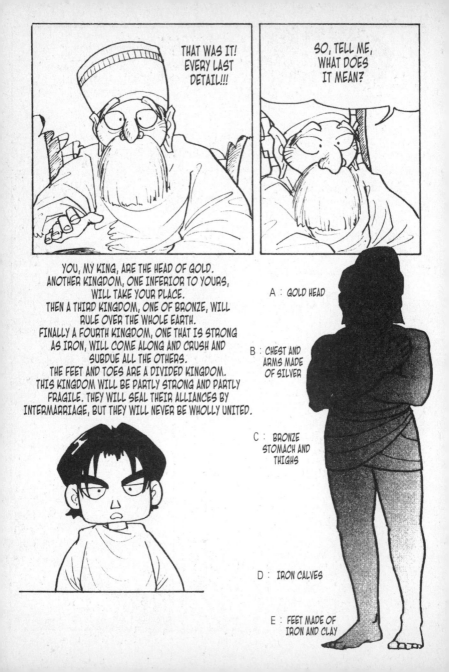

THAT WAS IT! EVERY LAST DETAIL!!!

SO, TELL ME, WHAT DOES IT MEAN?

YOU, MY KING, ARE THE HEAD OF GOLD. ANOTHER KINGDOM, ONE INFERIOR TO YOURS, WILL TAKE YOUR PLACE. THEN A THIRD KINGDOM, ONE OF BRONZE, WILL RULE OVER THE WHOLE EARTH. FINALLY A FOURTH KINGDOM, ONE THAT IS STRONG AS IRON, WILL COME ALONG AND CRUSH AND SUBDUE ALL THE OTHERS. THE FEET AND TOES ARE A DIVIDED KINGDOM. THIS KINGDOM WILL BE PARTLY STRONG AND PARTLY FRAGILE. THEY WILL SEAL THEIR ALLIANCES BY INTERMARRIAGE, BUT THEY WILL NEVER BE WHOLLY UNITED.

A : GOLD HEAD

B : CHEST AND ARMS MADE OF SILVER

C : BRONZE STOMACH AND THIGHS

D : IRON CALVES

E : FEET MADE OF IRON AND CLAY

SADLY, NEBUCHADNEZZAR GREW EVEN MORE PRIDEFUL AFTER WINNING MORE BATTLES AND MAKING BABYLON THE MOST POWERFUL NATION IN THE WORLD.

AM I A MAN...

... OR A GOD!?!

AH, THE GREATNESS I HAVE! SUCH STRENGTH! SO HANDSOME! HIGHLY EDUCATED! CHARISMATIC!

YES, I AM NOT HUMAN! I AM A GOD WHO RULES THE HUMAN WORLD!

I JUST CAN'T STOP THINKING ABOUT MYSELF AND HOW WONDERFUL I AM.

AM I A HUMAN OR A -- ?

KA-ZAP!

FOR SEVEN YEARS, NEBUCHADNEZZAR LIVED LIKE A WILD ANIMAL AND ROAMED THE FIELDS.

MEOW! I'M A KITTY-CAT. MEOW!

IN THE END, HE UNDERSTOOD THAT ALL AUTHORITY COMES FROM GOD AND THAT HE MUST GIVE GOD ALL THE GLORY. HE BECAME KING AGAIN.

I'M ONLY HUMAN.

DANIEL!
DANIEL!

DANIEL! ARE YOU DEAD?

NO, MY KING!
GOD CLOSED THE
MOUTH OF THE LIONS
AND SAVED ME.

END OF DANIEL

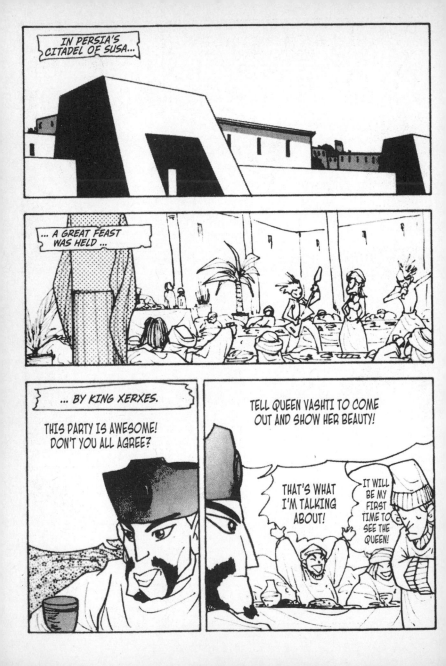

HOW CAN YOU ANGER GOD BY MARRYING GENTILES AND WORSHIPING IDOLS AFTER ALL THOSE YEARS OF EXILE?!?

STOP THIS INSANITY!

SO THE ISRAELITES DIVORCED THE GENTILE WOMEN, AND EZRA'S REVOLUTION BEGAN.

GRAPHIC NOVELS

CHECK OUT THESE OTHER Z GRAPHIC NOVELS!

I Was an Eighth-Grade Ninja
Available Now!

The Judge of God
Available Now!

Pyramid Peril
Available Now!

The Coming Storm
Available Now!

Advent
Available Now!

ZONDERVAN®

We want to hear from you. Please send your comments
about this book to us in care of zreview@zondervan.com. Thank you.

Grand Rapids, MI 49530
www.zonderkidz.com

ZONDERVAN.com/
AUTHORTRACKER
follow your favorite authors